SNOWMEN IN SUMMER

Story by Caleb Selby
Illustrations by Hollie Rickner

Jonas and Zane loved winter. They loved the frosty mornings and the cold evenings. They loved sledding on the hills near the family farm. They loved having snowball fights with the neighbors and making snow angels too. But they loved winter most of all because they loved to make snowmen! Nothing in the world made the boys happier than putting on their warm gloves and hats and treading outside to create wonderful snowmen. They were the best snowman makers in the entire neighborhood.

Every year the boys would make their snowmen bigger and better than before. Eventually they began to need ladders to finish their frosty creations because they were so big. They would even make the biggest snowman's top-hat out of old tractor tires because regular hats were just too small.

Every year, people would come from miles around just to see the brothers and their amazing collection of snowmen. They were always delighted to see the newest additions.

But every year without fail, the cold winter months would give way to summer sunshine and warmth which would bring an end to all their fun. Try and wish as they might, the boys could not keep winter from slipping away year after year.

As the winter chill would leave their farm pastures and fields, so too did the beautiful, white, fluffy snow disappear, leaving nothing behind but a muddy mess to remind them of all the fun they had experienced that winter.

"I wish we could build snowmen all the time," said Zane to his older brother as he plopped himself down on the pile of tractor tires that they had so carefully stacked up just a few months earlier.

"Why can't we?" Jonas exclaimed as he jumped to his feet and held up a ball of drippy mud.

Zane looked at his older brother curiously for just a moment before a smile slowly crept over his face.

The boys worked hard making their first summer snowman. They were quite happy with how he turned out, but their mother was not as excited about their brown snowman as they were.

"I don't mind you boys playing outside, but you can't get so dirty!" the mother told the boys firmly when they showed her their creation. "Now go play in the back yard. Dinner will be ready soon."

"Yes ma'am," the boys said in unison and wandered out to the backyard. When they got to the backyard, they spotted several large bales of hay stacked by the barn. They looked at each other and smiled.

The boys built a beautiful snowman out of the big round bales of hay. A collection of wildflowers for a scarf, some rocks for the face, and a pair of pitchforks completed their creation.

"I'm glad you boys are having fun, but you can't use all my hay for your projects," the boys' father said firmly when they showed him their latest snowman. "Now run along and help your Grandma. I think she's getting supper ready."

"Yes, sir!" the boys said together and walked out to the picnic table where their Grandma was busily preparing their meal.

Grandma's lunch was nothing short of inspirational for two boys with active imaginations and time on their hands. Watermelon, cantaloupe, apples and bananas; it was a summer snowman's dream!

They hurriedly constructed a table-sized snowman and finished it just as their grandma walked up to them holding a picnic basket.

"Look what we made for you!" Zane shouted out with a beaming smile.

Grandma smiled warmly but then shook her head. "I'm happy you boys are enjoying lunch, but why don't you try enjoying it with your bellies and not your hands?" she said and then kissed each boy on the forehead. "Now go fetch your folks. It's time to eat!"

"Yes, Grandma!" the boys said and ran to find their parents.

"You boys have had a busy day," their mother said to them with a smile.

"You've made some mighty fine snowmen," their father added proudly as he watched a cow take a big bite of the hay snowman. "Even the cow likes them!"

"I never would have guessed my summer fruit basket would have turned into a snowman," their grandma said with a shake of her head. "Now you boys must be tired. Time to get washed up and off to bed. No more snowmen today."

Jonas and Zane looked at each other, winked, and smiled.

The last snowman of the day was skillfully made by the best snowman makers in the county with pillows, blankets, and toys. It stood guard over the boys as they slowly drifted off to sleep.

As the brothers quietly slept, they dreamed of colder days, snow-covered fields, chilly air, and steaming mugs of hot chocolate. But until winter came back, they would just have to keep making snowmen in summer.

~THE END~

-Four Seasons-

Winter, Spring, Summer & Fall
What's your favorite season of all?
Summer is hot
Winter is not
Four seasons, different, each one a ball!

27311312R00015